Jack
and the
Beanstalk

retold and illustrated by
Lorinda Bryan Cauley

G. P. Putnam's Sons   New York

Text & illustrations copyright © 1983 by Lorinda Bryan Cauley.
All rights reserved. Published simultaneously in
Canada by General Publishing Co. Limited, Toronto.
Printed in the United States of America.
Library of Congress Cataloging in Publication Data
Cauley, Lorinda Bryan.
Jack and the beanstalk.
Summary: A boy climbs to the top of a giant beanstalk
where he uses his quick wits to outsmart a giant
and make his and his mother's fortune.
[1. Fairy tales. 2. Folklore—England.
3. Giants—Fiction] I. Title.
PZ8.C285Jak 1983 398.2' 1' 0941 [E] 83-4596
ISBN 0-399-20901-8
ISBN 0-399-20902-6 (pbk.)
First impression.

For my brother Gordon, who loves to grow things

There was once upon a time a poor widow who had an only son named Jack and a cow named Milky-White. All they had to live on was the milk the cow gave, which they carried to the market and sold.

But one morning Milky-White gave no milk. "What shall we do, what shall we do?" said Jack's mother, wringing her hands.

"Cheer up, Mother," said Jack. "It's market day today, and I'll soon sell Milky-White and then we'll see what we can do."

So he took the cow's halter in his hand and off he started.

Jack hadn't gone far when he met a funny-looking old man who said, "Good morning and where are you off to?"

"I'm going to market to sell our cow."

"Oh," said the man. "I don't mind doing a swap with you—your cow for these beans. If you plant them overnight, by morning they will grow right up to the sky."

"Really?" said Jack, amazed. And he handed over Milky-White.

When Jack arrived home, his mother asked, "Back already, Jack? How much did you get for Milky-White?"

"What do you say to these beans," Jack told her. "Plant them overnight and . . ."

"What!" said Jack's mother. "Have you been so foolish!" And she threw the beans out the window and sent Jack to bed without any supper.

The next morning when Jack woke up, the room looked funny. The sun was shining into part of it, but the rest was dark and shady. He jumped up and went to the window and what do you think he saw? Why, the beans had sprung up into a big beanstalk which went up and up and up like a ladder until it reached the sky.

Jack jumped onto the beanstalk and up he climbed until he reached the clouds and found a road stretching into the distance. He walked along it until he came to a great big tall house, and on the doorstep of the house was a great big tall woman.

"Good morning," said Jack. "Could you be so kind as to give me some breakfast?" For Jack had left home without anything to eat.

"If it's breakfast you want, it's breakfast you'll be," said the great big tall woman. "My man is a giant and there's nothing he likes better than boys broiled on toast."

"Oh, please give me something to eat," begged Jack. So the giant's wife, who was not half so bad, took Jack into the kitchen and gave him some bread and milk.

But Jack had just started to eat when there was a thump, thump, thump! And the whole house began to tremble with the noise of someone coming.

"Goodness gracious me! It's him," said the giant's wife. "What on earth shall I do? Come along quick and jump in here." And she bundled Jack into the oven just as the giant came in. He was a big one to be sure.

"Ah, what's this I smell!" he boomed.

Fee fi fo fum
I smell the blood of an Englishman.
Be he live, or be he dead,
I'll have his bones to grind my bread.

"Nonsense, dear," said the woman. "You smell the scraps of the little boy you liked so much for yesterday's dinner. You go and have a wash and by the time you come back your breakfast will be ready for you."

While the giant was off washing, Jack was about to jump out of the oven and run away when the woman whispered to him, "Wait till he's asleep. He always has a doze after breakfast."

Well, the giant came back and ate and when he had finished, he went to a big chest and took out a couple of bags of gold. He sat at the table and counted the gold until his head began to nod and he began to snore and the whole house began to shake.

Then Jack crept out on tiptoe from the oven, and as he was passing the giant, he took one of the bags of gold and off he ran with it under his arm.

When he reached the beanstalk, he threw the bag down into his mother's garden and climbed down after it.

Jack showed his mother the gold and said, "Well, Mother, wasn't I right about the beans? They are really magical, you see."

So they lived on the bag of gold for some time. But at last they came to the end of it and Jack made up his mind to try his luck once more.

So one fine day he got up early and jumped onto the beanstalk and he climbed and he climbed and he climbed until he came to the road again. And he went along to see the great big tall house where the woman and the giant lived. And there, sure enough, was the great big tall woman, standing on the doorstep.

"Good morning," said Jack. "Could you be so good as to give me something to eat?"

"Aren't you the boy who came here once before? Do you know that my husband missed one of his bags of gold that very day?"

"That's strange," said Jack. "I dare say I could tell you something about that, but I'm so hungry I can't speak till I've had something to eat."

Well, the big tall woman was so curious that she took Jack in and gave him something to eat. But Jack had scarcely begun munching when thump, thump, thump, they heard the giant's footsteps.

Away went Jack, into the oven to hide.

All happened as it did before. In came the giant, saying, "Fee fi fo fum." Then he demanded his breakfast, and after he had eaten, he said, "Wife, bring me the hen that lays the golden eggs."

So she brought it and the giant said, "Lay." And the hen laid an egg of gold. Then the giant began to nod his head and to snore until the house shook.

Jack crept out of the oven on tiptoe and caught hold of the hen and was off. But just as he was going out the door, the hen gave a cackle which woke the giant. Jack heard him calling, "Wife, wife, what have you done with my golden hen?"

But that was all Jack heard, for he rushed off to the beanstalk, climbed down it, and showed his mother the wonderful hen.

"Lay," he said, and the hen laid a golden egg.

But after a time, even though the hen laid a golden egg every time Jack said, "Lay," Jack was not content.

So one fine morning he got up early, jumped onto the beanstalk, and climbed to the top for the third time. But he knew better than to go straight to the giant's house and speak to the great big tall woman.

So he waited behind a bush till he saw the giant's wife come out with a pail to get some water. Then he crept into the house and got into a copper box on the table. He hadn't been there long when he heard thump, thump, thump, and in came the giant and his wife.

"Fee fi fo fum. I smell the blood of an English-man," cried out the giant. "I smell him, wife. I smell him."

"Do you, dearie?" said the wife. "Then if it's the little boy who stole your gold and your golden hen, he's sure to be hiding in the oven."

But Jack wasn't there, of course, and the giant's wife said, "There you go again with your fee fi fo fum. Why, of course, it's the boy you caught last night that I've just broiled for your breakfast."

So the giant sat down to eat, but every now and then he would mutter, "Well, I could have sworn . . ." And up he'd get and search every-where except in the copper box right under his nose.

After breakfast the giant called out, "Wife, wife, bring me my golden harp."

After she had put it on the table in front of him, the giant said, "Sing." And the golden harp sang most beautifully and it went on singing until the giant fell asleep and snored like thunder.

Then Jack lifted up the lid of the copper box and quietly crept on his hands and knees and caught hold of the golden harp. As he dashed with it toward the door, the harp called out loudly, "Master! Master!" and the giant woke up just in time to see Jack running off with his harp.

Jack ran as fast as he could, with the giant rushing after him. The giant was not more than twenty yards away when suddenly he saw Jack disappear. He looked down through the clouds and saw Jack climbing down the beanstalk.

Well, the giant didn't like trusting himself to such a ladder and he stood and watched until the harp cried out, "Master! Master!" And with that the giant swung himself onto the beanstalk and started down after Jack. The beanstalk swayed and creaked under his great weight.

By this time Jack had nearly reached the ground. "Mother, Mother," he called out. "Bring me an ax! Bring me an ax!"

His mother came rushing out with the ax in her hands. But when she came to the beanstalk, she stood still with fright. For there she saw the giant with his legs coming down the beanstalk through the clouds.

Jack grabbed the ax and gave a chop which cut the beanstalk in half. The giant felt the beanstalk shake and quiver and he looked down to see what was the matter. Then Jack gave another chop and the beanstalk was cut in two. The giant came tumbling down and the beanstalk came toppling after him.

Well, that was the end of the giant. And with the hen that laid golden eggs and a harp that sang, Jack and his mother had no more worries and they lived happily ever after.